A DORLING KINDERSLEY BOOK

Project editor Monica Byles
U.S. editor and researcher Mary Ann Lynch
Art editor Peter Radcliffe
Managing art editor Chris Scollen
Managing editor Jane Yorke
Production Neil Palfreyman and Susannah Straughan

Illustration Simone Boni/L.R. Galante
Corythosaurus **model** Jeremy Hunt/Centaur Studios
Model photography Dave King
Museum photography Lynton Gardiner
U.K. Consultant Dr. Angela Milner, The Natural
History Museum, London

First American Edition, 1993
10 9 8 7 6 5 4 3 2 1

Published in the United States by
Dorling Kindersley, Inc., 232 Madison Avenue
New York, New York 10016

Copyright © 1993 Dorling Kindersley Limited, London

Reproduced by Colourscan, Singapore
Printed and bound in Italy by Graphicom

Library of Congress Cataloging-in-Publication Data

Lindsay, William
    Corythosaurus / Lindsay, William. – 1st American ed.
        p.   cm.
    At head of title: American Museum of Natural History.
    Includes index.
    Summary: Text and illustrations describe the discovery and
excavation of corythosaurus fossils and examine what the evidence
suggests about its appearance and behavior.
    ISBN 1-56458-225-6
    1. Corythosaurus – Juvenile literature.   [1. Corythosaurus.
2. Dinosaurs.   3. Fossils.   4. Paleontology.]   I. American Museum
of Natural History.   II. Title.   III. Lindsay, William.
QE862.O65L56   1993
567.9'7–dc20
                                                                92-54309
                                                                CIP
                                                                AC

AMERICAN MUSEUM OF NATURAL HISTORY

Corythosaurus

William Lindsay

Consultant Mark Norell

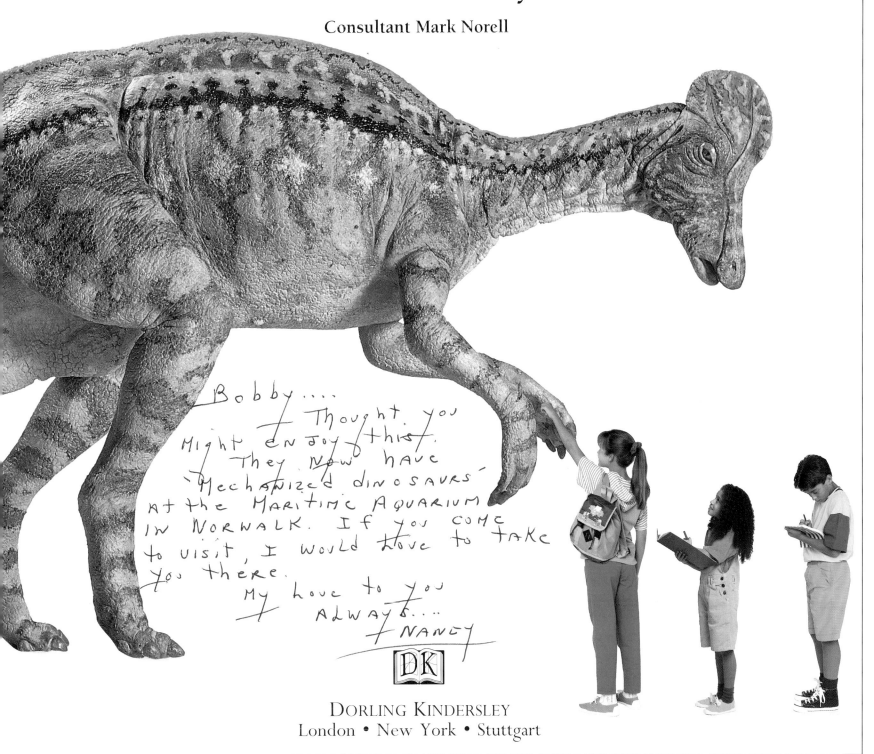

Bobby....
I Thought you
might enjoy this.
They now have
"Mechanized dinosaurs"
at the Maritime Aquarium
in Norwalk. If you come
to visit, I would love to take
you there.
My love to you
always....
† Nancy

DK

DORLING KINDERSLEY
London • New York • Stuttgart

Contents

INTRODUCTION

This book is about *Corythosaurus*, one of the many kinds of crested dinosaurs called hadrosaurs. For almost 90 million years, they may have traveled in herds eating plants, some similar to modern day pine trees. The fossilized remains of hadrosaurs have been collected on every continent except for Antarctica.

Hadrosaur fossils are likely to be found wherever there are rocks that were formed in the Late Cretaceous Period. These fossils tell us what dinosaurs might have been like when they were alive. I have collected fossils of closely related species in the Hell Creek Formation of North America, the Sahara Desert of West Africa, and the Gobi Desert of Mongolia. Because related hadrosaurs are found on different continents, the fossils suggest that some areas separated today by oceans may have been connected in the past.

Spectacular *Corythosaurus* specimens have been found, but we still have a great deal to learn. For instance, scientists do not know the function of the bony crest that gives this animal its name. Like so many questions in science, this may only be answered by future generations of paleontologists, scientists devoted to the study of fossils and life in ancient times.

Mark Norell
Assistant Curator of
Vertebrate Paleontology,
American Museum of Natural History

AGE OF THE DINOSAURS

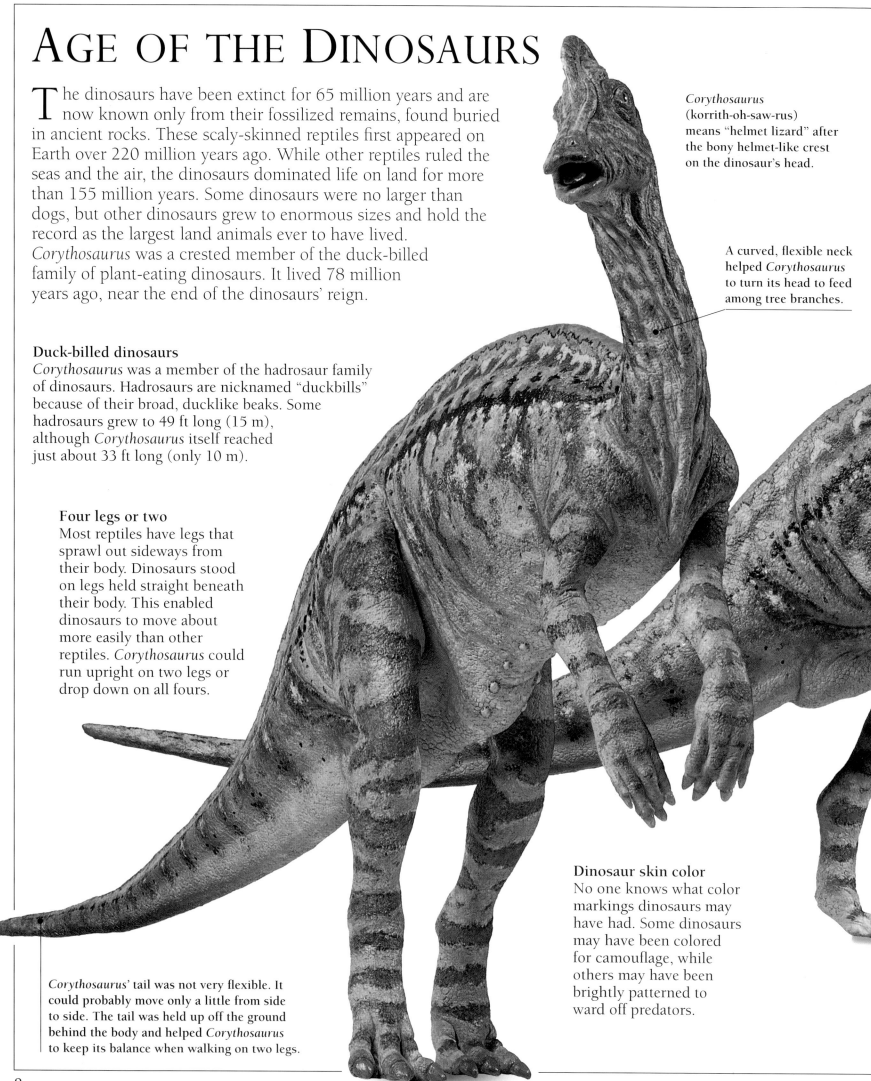

The dinosaurs have been extinct for 65 million years and are now known only from their fossilized remains, found buried in ancient rocks. These scaly-skinned reptiles first appeared on Earth over 220 million years ago. While other reptiles ruled the seas and the air, the dinosaurs dominated life on land for more than 155 million years. Some dinosaurs were no larger than dogs, but other dinosaurs grew to enormous sizes and hold the record as the largest land animals ever to have lived. *Corythosaurus* was a crested member of the duck-billed family of plant-eating dinosaurs. It lived 78 million years ago, near the end of the dinosaurs' reign.

Corythosaurus (korrith-oh-saw-rus) means "helmet lizard" after the bony helmet-like crest on the dinosaur's head.

A curved, flexible neck helped *Corythosaurus* to turn its head to feed among tree branches.

Duck-billed dinosaurs
Corythosaurus was a member of the hadrosaur family of dinosaurs. Hadrosaurs are nicknamed "duckbills" because of their broad, ducklike beaks. Some hadrosaurs grew to 49 ft long (15 m), although *Corythosaurus* itself reached just about 33 ft long (only 10 m).

Four legs or two
Most reptiles have legs that sprawl out sideways from their body. Dinosaurs stood on legs held straight beneath their body. This enabled dinosaurs to move about more easily than other reptiles. *Corythosaurus* could run upright on two legs or drop down on all fours.

Dinosaur skin color
No one knows what color markings dinosaurs may have had. Some dinosaurs may have been colored for camouflage, while others may have been brightly patterned to ward off predators.

Corythosaurus' tail was not very flexible. It could probably move only a little from side to side. The tail was held up off the ground behind the body and helped *Corythosaurus* to keep its balance when walking on two legs.

Knobby skin
Dinosaur skin was similar to that of reptiles living today, such as the crocodile. Fossil impressions found in rocks show that the skin was covered in thick, knobby bumps and scales.

The toothless beak and hundreds of grinding teeth are signs that *Corythosaurus* was a plant-eater, or herbivore. Fossilized plant remains, such as pine needles and cones, have been found with hadrosaur skeletons.

Hoof-shaped claws and padded toes show that the dinosaur's arms were mainly used for walking.

Two types of dinosaur
Corythosaurus was a "bird-hipped" or ornithischian dinosaur. Both of its lower hip bones pointed down and backward. "Lizard-hipped" or saurischian dinosaurs had one lower hip bone pointing down and forward, and the other down and backward.

Iguanodon
"bird-hipped" dinosaur

Plateosaurus
"lizard-hipped" dinosaur

Dinosaur times
Over millions of years, new kinds of dinosaurs replaced those that died out. *Corythosaurus* lived during the Earth's Cretaceous Period.

TRIASSIC PERIOD
245–208 million years ago

JURASSIC PERIOD
208–145 million years ago

CRETACEOUS PERIOD
145–65 million years ago

9

DINOSAUR DISCOVERY

In 1914, the famous dinosaur hunter, Barnum Brown, made a sensational find. He noticed fossil bones weathering out of rocks along the Red Deer River, near Steveville, Alberta, Canada. The bones were part of a beautifully preserved *Corythosaurus* skeleton – only the end of the tail and parts of the hands were missing.

Two years earlier, Brown had unearthed the first known specimen of *Corythosaurus*, but this second find was more complete. The bones were partly crushed, but they were still lying in their original positions, as if *Corythosaurus* had carefully lain down to die in soft, sandy mud, about 78 million years before.

Bones to stones
When animals and plants are buried underground, they are sometimes changed into hard replicas of themselves, called fossils. This change may take place over millions of years as chemicals in rocks and soil seep into the buried object.

1 Food and drink
About 78 million years ago, *Corythosaurus* pauses by a winding stream on a wide, flat plain. It feasts on the conifers, ferns, and flowers that grow there.

2 Muddy waters
A few years later, *Corythosaurus* lies dead on the bank of a river. The rains falling in the distant mountains will soon flood the river, sweeping mud and sand over the animal carcass.

3 Buried dinosaur
Over hundreds of years, the rivers move back and forward across the plain, building up layers of mud and sand over the buried skeleton. Other dinosaurs now live above ground.

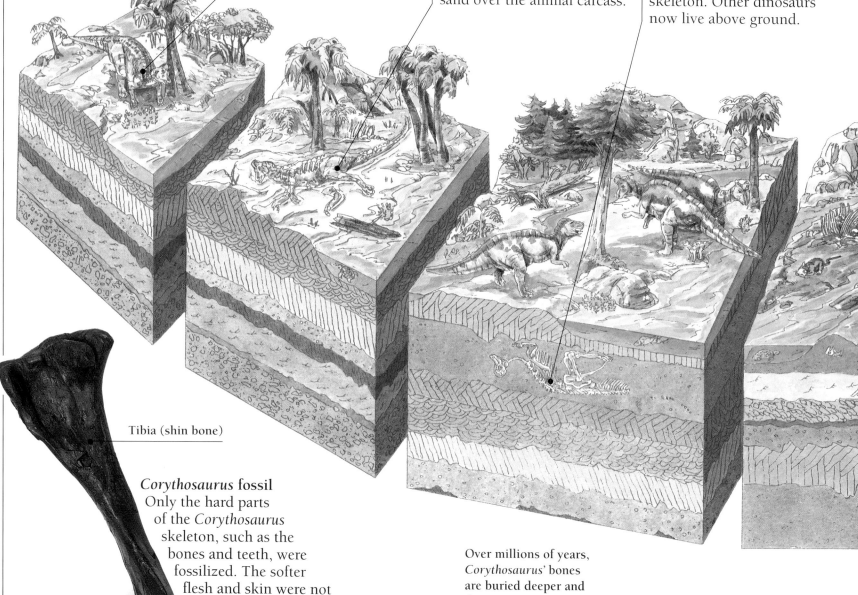

Tibia (shin bone)

Corythosaurus fossil
Only the hard parts of the *Corythosaurus* skeleton, such as the bones and teeth, were fossilized. The softer flesh and skin were not preserved, but rotted away in the damp soil soon after the dinosaur's death.

Over millions of years, *Corythosaurus'* bones are buried deeper and deeper underground.

DINOSAUR DETECTIVE

Barnum Brown (1873 – 1963)

Barnum Brown was one of the world's greatest dinosaur hunters. He found his first dinosaur fossil, a *Triceratops* skull, in 1895 and went on to fill the American Museum of Natural History (AMNH) in New York with many finds.

1873 Born in Carbondale, Kansas.
1897 Joined AMNH as a paleontologist, age 24.
1902 Discovered the first known remains of **Tyrannosaurus rex**.
1910 Leads expedition to hunt dinosaurs by boat along the Red Deer River, Alberta, Canada.
1912 Discovered the first **Corythosaurus** near Steveville, Alberta.
1914 Discovered a more complete specimen of **Corythosaurus**.
1963 Died in New York, at the age of 89.

Barnum Brown (to the right) on his flatboat on the Red Deer River

Dinosaur Provincial Park

Over 350 fossil skeletons, including that of *Corythosaurus*, have been found near the Red Deer River in Alberta, Canada. So many have been discovered that the area has been set aside as a dinosaur park.

Discovery site of *Corythosaurus*

Red Deer River, near Steveville, Alberta, Canada

4 Death of the dinosaurs

65 million years ago, the dinosaurs have become extinct. The skeleton slowly turns to fossil as chemicals pass from the rocks into the bones.

5 Cold world

15 thousand years ago, an ice age has spread over much of North America. Huge earth movements have pushed the rocks and the fossilized bones closer to the surface.

6 Exposed bones

Thousands of years of wind and rain have carved the rocks of the ancient riverbed into hills and gulleys. A few bones of the fossilized *Corythosaurus* have weathered out of the steep side of a canyon.

FRAGILE FIND

In 1909, Barnum Brown visited a ranch near the Red Deer River in Alberta, Canada. The ranch owner had found fossils high up in the barren canyons near his home. Brown identified the fossils as dinosaur bones and mounted an expedition on behalf of his employer, the American Museum of Natural History in New York.

Between 1910 and 1915, Barnum Brown and his team of dinosaur hunters used a flatboat, or barge, to travel down the river, going ashore to look for fossils in the nearby cliffs. In the summer of 1914, Brown and his colleagues excavated their best find, the well-preserved skeleton of an adult *Corythosaurus*.

1 Hunter's camp

Far from any town, the fossil hunters had to sleep in tents on the riverbank. Life was harsh, and the men often wore nets over their heads to protect them from mosquito bites. All meals were cooked in a tent on the flatboat. Each day, the team sailed farther down the river, stopping to go ashore and explore the steep canyons along the riverbanks.

2 Hard labor

In 1914, Brown noticed some fossil bones on an exposed rockface. Brown and his team began to dig the rock from around the bones. Before long, he had uncovered the nearly complete skeleton of a *Corythosaurus*.

When the rock was cleared away, the tailbones were found still connected.

3 Fossil discovery

After months of backbreaking work, the fragile fossils of *Corythosaurus* were finally uncovered. The fossils were riddled with cracks and gaps, but the shapes of the animal's limbs and tail were visible. Still partly attached to lumps of rock, the crumbling bones were carefully painted with glue to preserve their shape.

5 Heavy fossils

The huge blocks of rock and plaster containing the *Corythosaurus* skeleton were too heavy to lift by hand. Wooden beams, ropes, and pulleys were used to lift the massive blocks, lower them into strong, straw-lined crates, and then load them onto horse-drawn wagons.

4 Broken bones

Each block of rock containing the fragile fossils was wrapped in a protective jacket of plaster and burlap for the long journey to the museum in New York. The jackets would be removed when scientists began to prepare the bones for museum display.

The bones of the dinosaur's spine and neck, still covered with stone.

Part of the dinosaur's skeleton still lies buried.

6 Wagon train

The difficult journey by horse and cart to the railroad station often took many days. Many tons of fossils were carried in this way over the rough, barren landscape.

The arm bones have been well preserved, but parts of the hand were lost before the animal's carcass was buried.

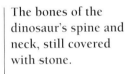

Rear leg of *Corythosaurus*

The bones of the right leg and foot partly conceal those on the other side.

7 Skeleton restoration

Back at the museum in New York, scientists first removed the plaster jackets from the broken bones, then glued them together and filled the gaps with plaster. Years of work were needed to transform the fossil fragments into an almost-perfect dinosaur skeleton.

SKELETON STORY

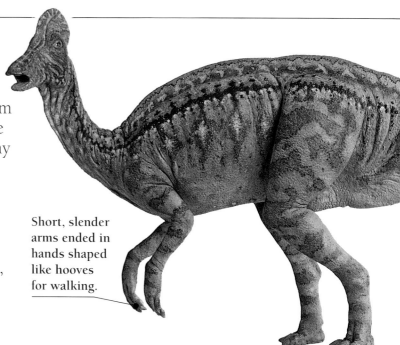

The nearly complete skeleton of *Corythosaurus* that Barnum Brown had excavated was finally placed on display at the American Museum of Natural History in New York after many years of painstaking restoration. Each fossil bone had to be chipped free of the surrounding rock, repaired with plaster, and strengthened with glue. The huge, 23 ft-long (7.5 m) skeleton was then put together and mounted in its original burial position in a large glass display case.

The skeleton can be identified as *Corythosaurus* by its skull, with a high, flat-sided crest; many rows of teeth; and horny beak. The powerful rear legs would have helped even a large adult *Corythosaurus* to run quite swiftly over short distances, to escape a prowling predator.

Short, slender arms ended in hands shaped like hooves for walking.

Death of a dinosaur
Lying on its side, the mounted skeleton captures the moment, millions of years ago, when sand and mud covered the dead body of *Corythosaurus*. The legs, arms, and body shape have been preserved almost undisturbed in the dinosaur's original death pose.

There were over 60 vertebrae in the tail.

Missing parts of the tail may have been washed away by floodwaters before the carcass was buried.

Bony corset
Like bird-hipped dinosaurs, *Corythosaurus* had extra scaffolding supporting its body. Long, bony rods, formed from muscle and tendons, crisscrossed along its backbone, over the hips, and into the tail. This bony corset helped *Corythosaurus* to walk upright on two legs but also held its tail stiff, so that it did not swing from side to side.

The long shaft of the ischium (rear hip bone) pointed backward far under the tail.

The large, three-toed feet ended in flattened hooves.

The stiff, straight tail helped to balance the dinosaur's body when moving on two legs.

Flat-sided, rounded crest of bone

Corythosaurus held the main part of its body level with the ground.

Two legs or four

A light, young *Corythosaurus* could walk easily on its hind legs, but a fully grown, heavy adult would have spent most of its time on all fours. When an adult *Corythosaurus* needed to escape an attacker, it could lift up its front limbs and run off quickly on its back legs.

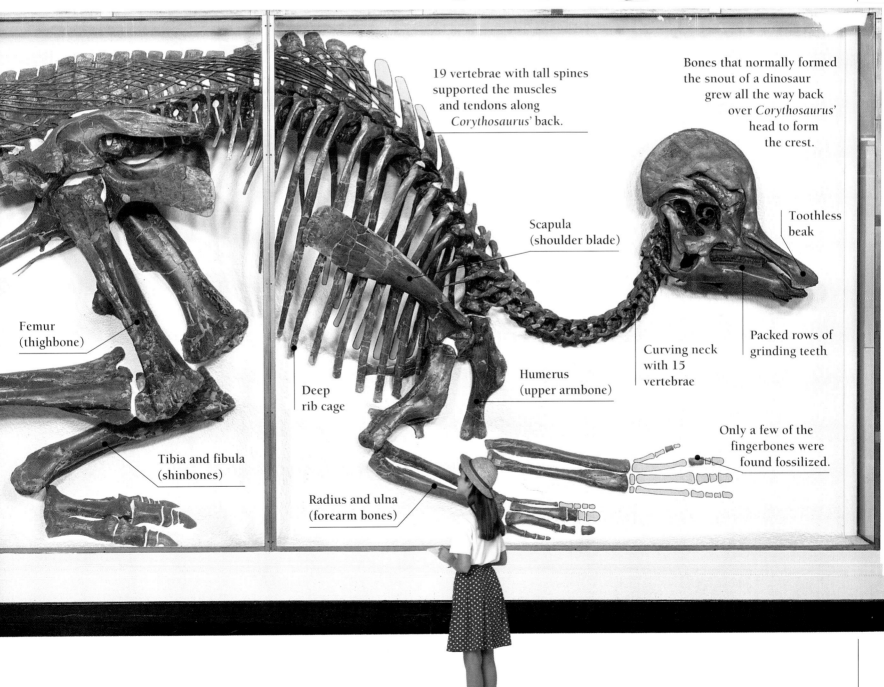

19 vertebrae with tall spines supported the muscles and tendons along *Corythosaurus'* back.

Bones that normally formed the snout of a dinosaur grew all the way back over *Corythosaurus'* head to form the crest.

Scapula (shoulder blade)

Toothless beak

Femur (thighbone)

Deep rib cage

Humerus (upper armbone)

Curving neck with 15 vertebrae

Packed rows of grinding teeth

Tibia and fibula (shinbones)

Radius and ulna (forearm bones)

Only a few of the fingerbones were found fossilized.

GREEDY GRAZER

During the Late Cretaceous Period, hadrosaurs like the 4-ton (4-tonne) *Corythosaurus* were among the most common dinosaurs of their day. Walking and running on powerful limbs, the duckbills may have traveled in large, fast-moving herds far across the coastal plains of what is now North America. These hungry plant-eaters munched their way through forest after forest of pine trees, ferns, flowers, and broad-leaved trees. Their rows of tightly packed teeth could mash even the toughest twigs into soft pulp, which was easy to swallow and digest.

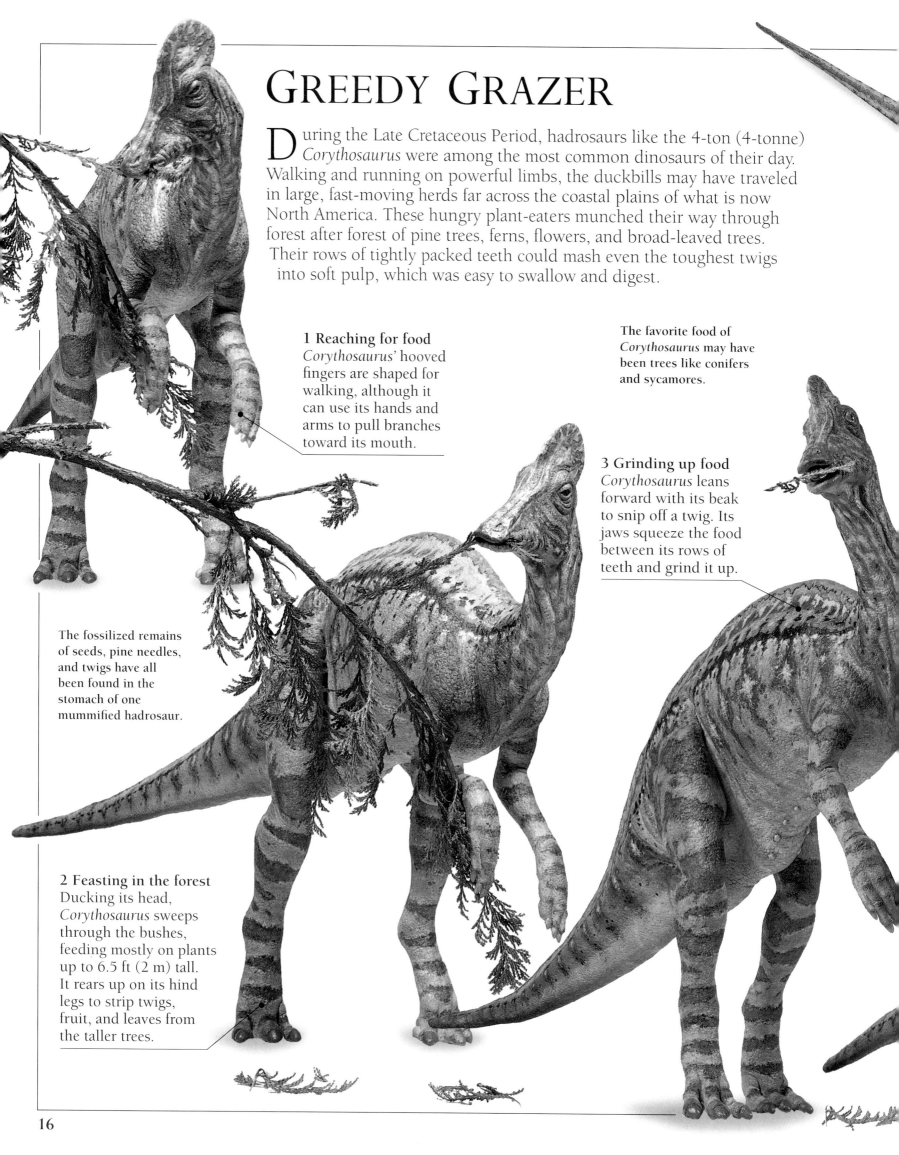

1 Reaching for food
Corythosaurus' hooved fingers are shaped for walking, although it can use its hands and arms to pull branches toward its mouth.

The favorite food of *Corythosaurus* may have been trees like conifers and sycamores.

3 Grinding up food
Corythosaurus leans forward with its beak to snip off a twig. Its jaws squeeze the food between its rows of teeth and grind it up.

The fossilized remains of seeds, pine needles, and twigs have all been found in the stomach of one mummified hadrosaur.

2 Feasting in the forest
Ducking its head, *Corythosaurus* sweeps through the bushes, feeding mostly on plants up to 6.5 ft (2 m) tall. It rears up on its hind legs to strip twigs, fruit, and leaves from the taller trees.

Corythosaurus' stiff tail did not swing from side to side, perhaps helping it to run fast.

A heavy adult *Corythosaurus* would most often stand and walk on all fours. But at the first sign of danger, it might rise on its back legs, with tail and body held straight, and perhaps run off at speeds from 9 to 12 mph (14 to 20 km/h).

Winter fodder

Remains of duck-billed dinosaurs have been found as far north as present-day Alaska. Few plants would have grown here in winter, so duck-billed dinosaurs may have migrated south to warmer areas, in search of fresh food to satisfy their appetite.

4 Moving off

Corythosaurus stands upright to strip the last branches that it can reach. The trees are left with torn bark and bare branches. It is time for the dinosaur to move on to new feeding grounds.

No fossil evidence shows the original skin color of *Corythosaurus*, but it may have had striking markings, like some birds and reptiles today.

Scientists once thought that *Corythosaurus* had webbed hands. Fossil evidence has revealed that each finger was padded with a tough, fleshy cushion.

SIGHT AND SMELL

The duckbills, or hadrosaurs, are among the most easily identified of all the dinosaurs. Many of the species, including *Corythosaurus*, were distinguished by spectacular head crests and distinctive mouths. *Corythosaurus'* sharp, rough-edged beak, which may have grown throughout the animal's life, was probably made of horn over bone, like human fingernails. The dinosaur's interlocking rows of teeth were also constantly replaced with new teeth, growing up from the jaw as the old ones wore down. As a group, the hadrosaur family probably had highly developed senses of sight, smell, and hearing to help them pick up messages from other dinosaurs, such as a warning of danger from an approaching predator.

Dinosaur senses
Although the brain of *Corythosaurus* seems small for such a large animal, it was well developed. It controlled the senses of sight, smell, and hearing as well as other body functions.

Chamber with smell-detecting part of the brain

Air passage to crest

Brain connected to smell organs

Nostrils let air into the hollow crest.

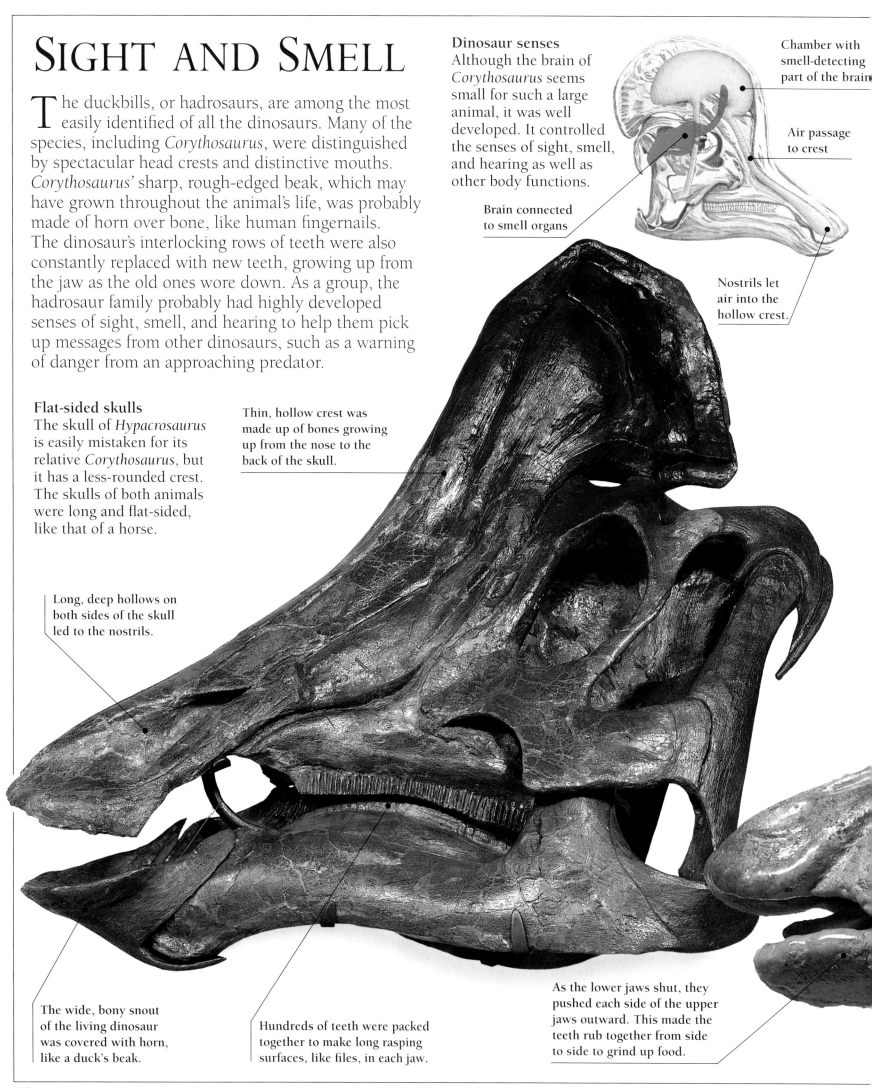

Flat-sided skulls
The skull of *Hypacrosaurus* is easily mistaken for its relative *Corythosaurus*, but it has a less-rounded crest. The skulls of both animals were long and flat-sided, like that of a horse.

Thin, hollow crest was made up of bones growing up from the nose to the back of the skull.

Long, deep hollows on both sides of the skull led to the nostrils.

The wide, bony snout of the living dinosaur was covered with horn, like a duck's beak.

Hundreds of teeth were packed together to make long rasping surfaces, like files, in each jaw.

As the lower jaws shut, they pushed each side of the upper jaws outward. This made the teeth rub together from side to side to grind up food.

Dinosaur vision

Many predators have eyes that face forward, giving them good vision for hunting or for using their hands.

Like many plant-eating animals, *Corythosaurus* had large eyes on the sides of its head. It could see in two different directions at once and watch for danger over a wide area as it fed.

Scientists do not know, however, if *Corythosaurus* saw in color, as people do, or in shades of gray.

Corythosaurus would have seen two separate views of its surroundings at the same time. Its brain made sense of the different view from each side of its head.

The left eye sees a *Euoplocephalus* feeding in the vegetation.

The right eye sees danger from a hungry, prowling *Albertosaurus*.

Left eye

Right eye

Head signals

Hadrosaurs may have been able to recognize family members from the color markings on their heads and from the differently shaped skulls. They communicated by using the air chambers in their crests to make distinctive hoots and calls.

The bony crest was covered in skin and may have been highly patterned to help hadrosaurs recognize others from the same group.

All *Corythosaurus* crests were flat-sided, but some were smaller than others. Males may have had larger crests than females.

A large eardrum at the back of the head may have helped *Corythosaurus* to hear calls made by other dinosaurs in the area.

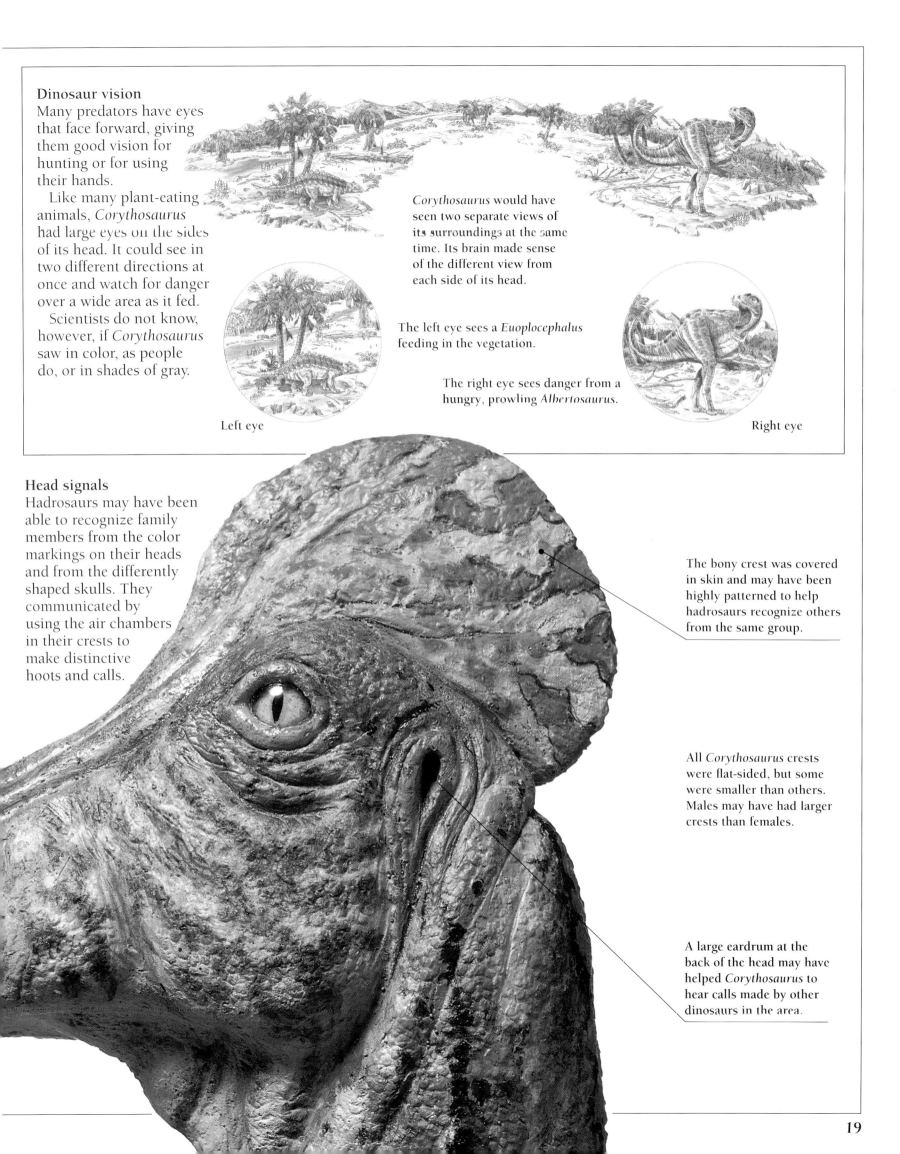

HORNBLOWERS

F ew living animals can compete with the amazing head crests sported by the hadrosaur family. Scientists once thought that hadrosaur crests were used as underwater snorkels and airtanks, or that they helped the dinosaurs to smell an approaching attacker. Hadrosaurs could tell males from females, and young dinosaurs from old, by the distinctive size and shape of their crests.

In recent experiments, scientists have tried blowing air through tubes similar to those in hollow hadrosaur crests. Results show that some duckbills could use their crests to call to one another.

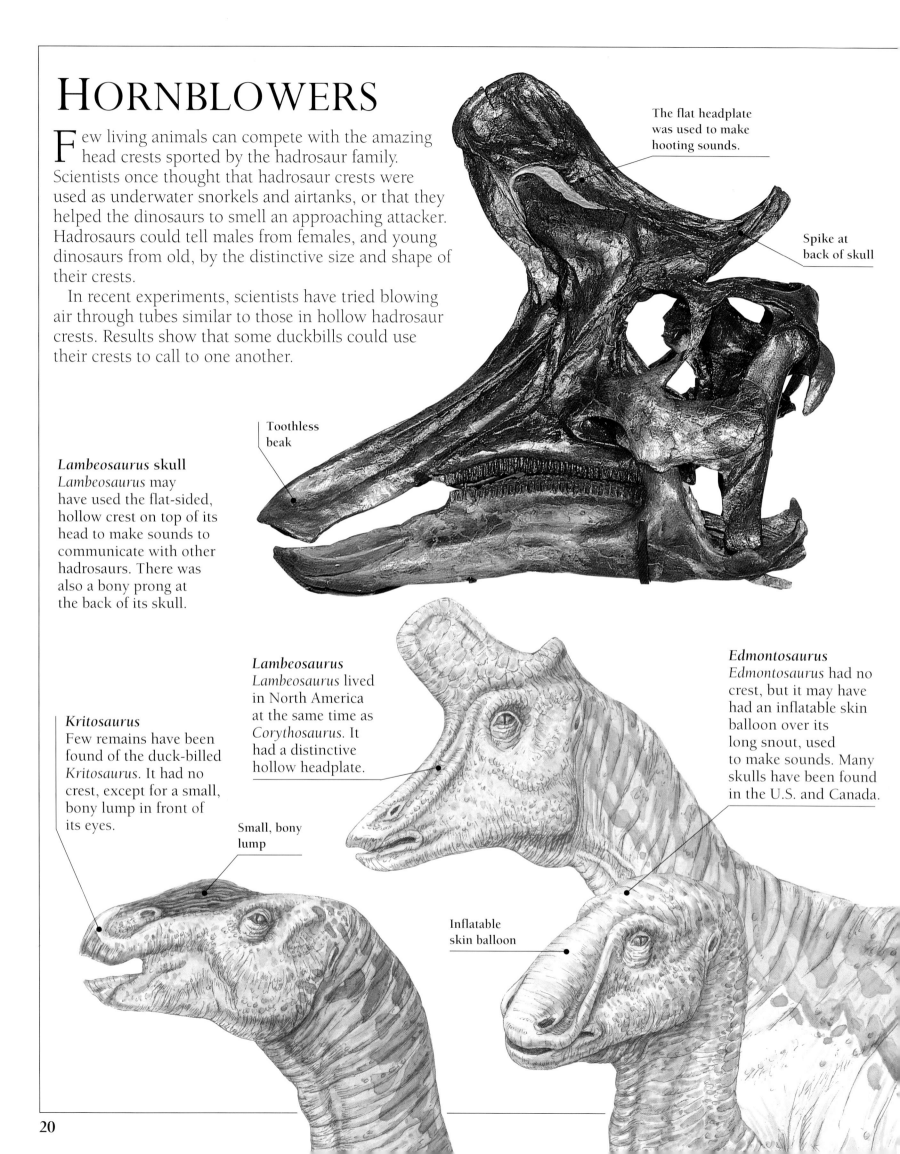

The flat headplate was used to make hooting sounds.

Spike at back of skull

Toothless beak

Lambeosaurus skull
Lambeosaurus may have used the flat-sided, hollow crest on top of its head to make sounds to communicate with other hadrosaurs. There was also a bony prong at the back of its skull.

Kritosaurus
Few remains have been found of the duck-billed *Kritosaurus*. It had no crest, except for a small, bony lump in front of its eyes.

Small, bony lump

Lambeosaurus
Lambeosaurus lived in North America at the same time as *Corythosaurus*. It had a distinctive hollow headplate.

Inflatable skin balloon

Edmontosaurus
Edmontosaurus had no crest, but it may have had an inflatable skin balloon over its long snout, used to make sounds. Many skulls have been found in the U.S. and Canada.

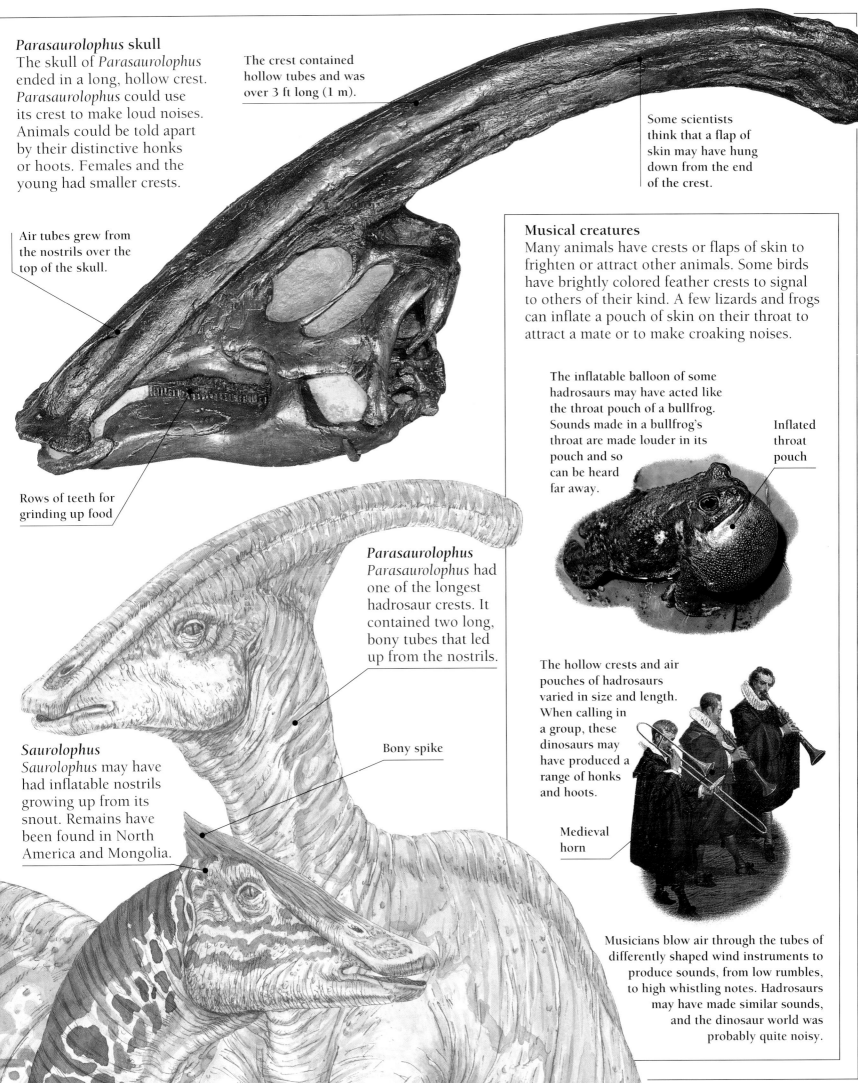

Parasaurolophus skull
The skull of *Parasaurolophus* ended in a long, hollow crest. *Parasaurolophus* could use its crest to make loud noises. Animals could be told apart by their distinctive honks or hoots. Females and the young had smaller crests.

The crest contained hollow tubes and was over 3 ft long (1 m).

Some scientists think that a flap of skin may have hung down from the end of the crest.

Air tubes grew from the nostrils over the top of the skull.

Musical creatures
Many animals have crests or flaps of skin to frighten or attract other animals. Some birds have brightly colored feather crests to signal to others of their kind. A few lizards and frogs can inflate a pouch of skin on their throat to attract a mate or to make croaking noises.

Rows of teeth for grinding up food

The inflatable balloon of some hadrosaurs may have acted like the throat pouch of a bullfrog. Sounds made in a bullfrog's throat are made louder in its pouch and so can be heard far away.

Inflated throat pouch

Parasaurolophus
Parasaurolophus had one of the longest hadrosaur crests. It contained two long, bony tubes that led up from the nostrils.

Saurolophus
Saurolophus may have had inflatable nostrils growing up from its snout. Remains have been found in North America and Mongolia.

Bony spike

The hollow crests and air pouches of hadrosaurs varied in size and length. When calling in a group, these dinosaurs may have produced a range of honks and hoots.

Medieval horn

Musicians blow air through the tubes of differently shaped wind instruments to produce sounds, from low rumbles, to high whistling notes. Hadrosaurs may have made similar sounds, and the dinosaur world was probably quite noisy.

DINOSAUR MUMMY

In August 1908, George and Levi Sternberg, brothers from a family of dinosaur hunters, made an amazing discovery in the sandstone hills of Wyoming. They unearthed the first dinosaur mummy ever found – an *Edmontosaurus*, still wrapped in the impression of its skin. Millions of years before, hot weather had dried the dinosaur's body, which was then buried and slowly turned into fossil.

In 1912, near the Red Deer River in Alberta, Canada, Barnum Brown found another important duck-billed specimen – the skin-covered fossil skeleton of a *Corythosaurus*.

Dinosaur skin to fossil impression
The carcass of the *Corythosaurus* specimen found by Brown was probably carried away by floods and left stranded on a sandbank in a river. As the waters subsided, deep layers of sand and silt settled on top of the dead dinosaur.

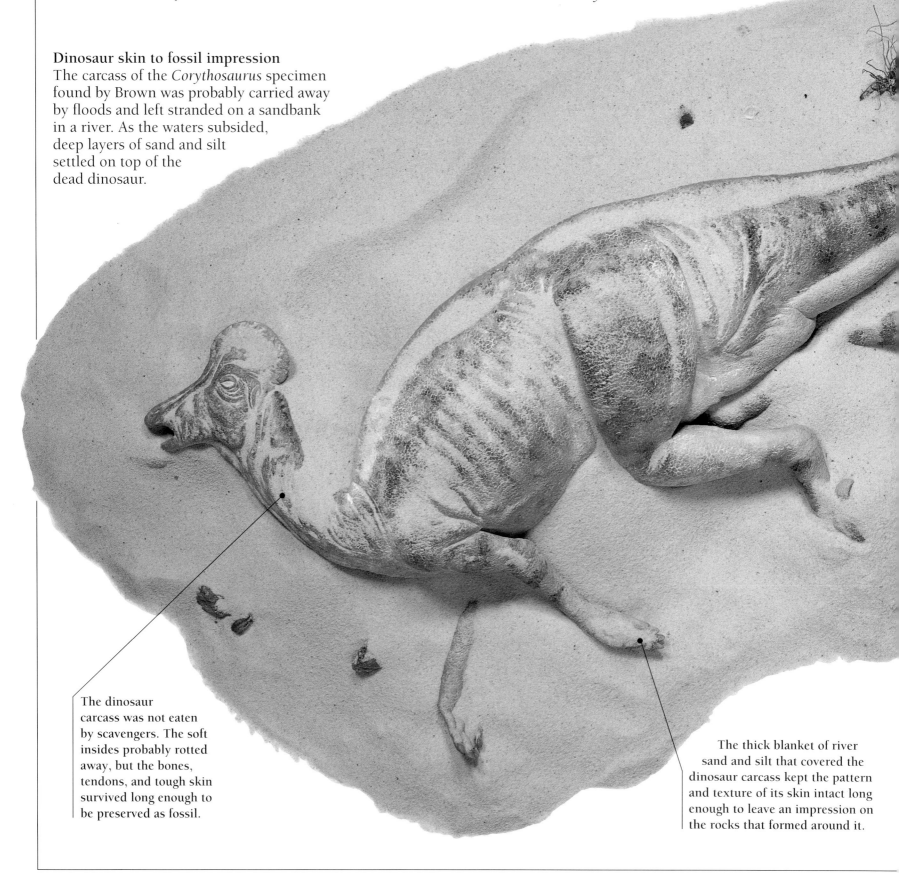

The dinosaur carcass was not eaten by scavengers. The soft insides probably rotted away, but the bones, tendons, and tough skin survived long enough to be preserved as fossil.

The thick blanket of river sand and silt that covered the dinosaur carcass kept the pattern and texture of its skin intact long enough to leave an impression on the rocks that formed around it.

Cousin of *Corythosaurus*

Edmontosaurus was another member of the duck-billed, or hadrosaur, family. Unlike *Corythosaurus*, it had a flat skull but may have had an inflatable pouch of skin over its snout to make calling sounds. *Edmontosaurus* lived slightly later than *Corythosaurus* in the same area, now known as North America, and was one of the last surviving dinosaurs.

The dinosaur's soft flesh rotted away, leaving a perfect imprint in the surrounding rock. Over millions of years, chemicals in the hardening sand and silt slowly turned the buried *Corythosaurus* bones into stony fossils.

Edmontosaurus fossil mummy

The mummified *Edmontosaurus* was found by the Sternberg family in Niobrara County, Wyoming. It gave scientists the first evidence that dinosaur skin was similar to that of living reptiles. This specimen is now on display at the AMNH.

Skin print

This fossilized impression, found by Barnum Brown, clearly shows that *Corythosaurus* skin was covered in a mosaic of small, pebbly bumps. But it cannot tell us what color the markings on the dinosaur's body may have been.

Dry heat made the tendons of the *Edmontosaurus* carcass shrink. The body twisted, with its legs and ribs in the air, and its head pulled back behind the shoulders.

RIVERSIDE FEAST

About 78 million years ago, *Corythosaurus* foraged along a broad, flat plain crisscrossed by swamps and rivers. This plain lay along the western shores of a great sea that washed from north to south across the middle of the land that is now called North America.

Many other plant-eating and meat-eating dinosaurs roamed through the vast forests with *Corythosaurus*. The plant-eaters fed on ferns and trees including conifers, cypresses, and flowering magnolias, which flourished amidst the waterlogged swamps and river channels.

Dinosaur heaven
The lush forests and rivers attracted many kinds of dinosaurs. Numerous plants grew to feed the herds of hungry herbivores, and there was a large supply of fresh water to drink. Lone meat-eaters, or carnivores, such as *Albertosaurus*, prowled the area, hoping to catch a young or sickly plant-eater.

Watching out for danger
Corythosaurus may have had excellent senses of sight, smell, and hearing. At the first sign of danger from a predator, it could sound the alarm with a booming, loud hoot from its high, crested head.

Running away
Corythosaurus enjoyed a diet of palm leaves, pine needles, fruits, and seeds. But at the first sign of a predator, it would quickly end its feast and rise up on its hind legs to escape.

Duckbills may have paddled through the rivers and swamps, feeding on overhanging branches. Sometimes, the water may have been the only place to escape from an attacking predator.

After the hadrosaurs, the horned dinosaurs were the second largest group by the riverside. Single-horned *Centrosaurus* could defend itself against attack with its sharp horns.

Away from the riverbank, a group of *Lambeosaurus* would have watched nervously for the approach of a prowling *Albertosaurus*.

Ferocious hunter
Fierce *Albertosaurus* hunted by the river. Its razor-sharp teeth could slash the soft flesh of its victims, the plant-eaters.

Euoplocephalus was well armored against *Albertosaurus*.

Group defense
Chasmosaurus used its long, sharp brow horns in defense against an *Albertosaurus*. In times of danger, a herd of *Chasmosaurus* might have formed a circle for protection and turned, horns outward, to face their attacker.

Poor swimmer
In the past, researchers believed that *Corythosaurus* could swim by waving its tail to and fro in the water, like a crocodile. Fossil evidence shows that a cage of bony rods held its back and tail rigid so that it could not swim. In fact, *Corythosaurus* could only paddle in shallow river waters.

A young *Corythosaurus* prepares to run for its life.

CORYTHOSAURUS FACT FILE

- **Specimen number:** AMNH 5338
- **Excavated by:** Barnum Brown
- **Excavation:** 1914, near Steveville, along the Red Deer River, Alberta, Canada
- **Bones found:** Complete skeleton, except for a few handbones and some tailbones
- **Where displayed:** American Museum of Natural History (AMNH), New York
- **Constructed:** Mounted as a half-skeleton

- **Lived:** About 78 million years ago, during the Cretaceous Period
- **Family:** Hadrosaurids, the duck-billed dinosaurs
- **Dinosaur type:** Bird-hipped (ornithischian)
- **Diet:** Plant matter, such as leaves, fruit, and seeds
- **Weight when alive:** Over 4 tons (about 4 tonnes)
- **Height:** Approximately 10 ft (3 m)
- **Length:** Approximately 24 ft (7.5 m)
- **Top speed:** Possibly over 31 mph (up to 50 km/h)

🏛 ON THE MUSEUM TRAIL 🏛

A museum guide to hadrosaurid specimens
A partial listing of both fossils and replica casts of fossils.

UNITED STATES

(*Edmontosaurus, Maiasaura, Parasaurolophus*) University of California Museum of Paleontology, Berkeley, California

(*Maiasaura*) Museum of the Rockies, Bozeman, Montana

(*Lambeosaurus*) Field Museum of Natural History, Chicago, Illinois

(*Corythosaurus, Edmontosaurus, Lambeosaurus, Saurolophus*) American Museum of Natural History, New York

(*Corythosaurus, Edmontosaurus*) National Museum of Natural History, Smithsonian Institution, Washington, D.C.

CANADA

(*Corythosaurus, Edmontosaurus, Kritosaurus, Lambeosaurus, Parasaurolophus, Prosaurolophus*) Royal Ontario Museum, Toronto, Ontario

(*Corythosaurus, Hadrosaurus, Hypacrosaurus, Lambeosaurus, Maiasaura, Prosaurolophus*) Tyrrell Museum of Paleontology, Drumheller, Alberta

Hadrosaurid specimens may also be found in museums in Argentina, China, France, Germany, Japan, Mongolia, Poland, Russia, Sweden, Taiwan, and the United Kingdom.

Cased dinosaur
Corythosaurus is displayed at the AMNH in its original death pose.

Corythosaurus had a strange helmeted head. It lived 78 million years ago in the land now known as North America.

Around the world

Hadrosaurid dinosaurs once lived all around the world. Their fossils have been found on almost every continent, from Alaska in the North, to Argentina in the South. The nests, eggs, and young of hadrosaurs have been found as well as entire skeletons.

Key to map

1 *Corythosaurus*
2 *Edmontosaurus*
3 *Kritosaurus*
4 *Lambeosaurus*
5 *Parasaurolophus*
6 *Saurolophus*

Family members

Corythosaurus is a member of the hadrosaur family, or duck-billed dinosaurs. These were all members of a larger group called the ornithopods.

Parasaurolophus lived at about the same time as *Corythosaurus* and in the same areas.

Lambeosaurus was larger than *Corythosaurus* and also lived in the Late Cretaceous Period and in the same parts of North America.

One of the last of the duck-billed dinosaurs, *Saurolophus* had a spiked head crest and, unlike *Corythosaurus*, lived in both Asia and North America.

Flat-headed *Edmontosaurus* is one of the most common fossil finds among hadrosaurs. It lived in North America, later than *Corythosaurus*, and was over 49 ft in length (13 m).

Kritosaurus was over 29 ft long (9 m). It had one of the simplest head shapes of the hadrosaurs. Only a bump in front of its eyes stood out on its flat head.

27

GLOSSARY

carcass
The dead body of an animal.

carnivore
A meat-eating animal.

crest
A decoration of feathers, skin, or bone growing on top of an animal's head, and perhaps used to attract attention from other animals of its kind.

Cretaceous Period
Part of the Earth's history, which lasted from 145 million years ago until the dinosaurs died out 65 million years ago. *Corythosaurus* lived during this period.

dinosaurs
A group of extinct, land reptiles that lived on Earth from 230 until 65 million years ago.

excavate
To dig up an object such as a fossil.

extinction
When living things, such as dinosaurs, die out and disappear from the Earth forever.

fossil
Part of a dead plant or animal that has been buried and then slowly turned as hard as stone by chemicals in the rock.

hadrosaur
Another name for a duck-billed dinosaur, such as *Corythosaurus*.

herbivore
A plant-eating animal.

Jurassic Period
Part of the Earth's history from 208 to 145 million years ago, when large plant-eating dinosaurs were common.

mosaic
A pattern made up of small pieces.

mummy
A carcass that has been dried out by wind and sun before being buried and, as a result, been kept from rotting.

ornithischian dinosaur
The bird-hipped type of dinosaur with both lower hip bones pointing down and backward.

ornithopods
A group of plant-eating dinosaurs that normally walked on two legs.

paleontologist
A scientist who studies fossils and life in ancient times.

pelvis
The group of bones where the legs join the backbone of an animal's skeleton.

replica
A copy of something.

reptile
A scaly animal that lays eggs, such as the turtles, snakes, lizards, and crocodiles of today. Dinosaurs were reptiles.

saurischian dinosaur
The lizard-hipped type of dinosaur with one of two lower hip bones pointing down and forward; the other bone pointing down and backward.

skeleton
The supporting bony frame inside an animal's body.

specimen
One example of a kind of plant or animal, or a part of it.

Triassic Period
Part of the Earth's history, which lasted from 245 to 208 million years ago, during which the dinosaurs first appeared.

vertebrae
Bones that form the backbone of animals.

weathering
When rocks and soil are broken up and washed or blown away by wind, rain, sun, frost, and other weather.

Pronunciation guide to the dinosaur names in this book

- *Albertosaurus* (al-bert-oh-saw-rus)
- *Centrosaurus* (sen-tro-saw-rus)
- *Corythosaurus* (korrith-oh-saw-rus)
- *Edmontosaurus* (ed-mon-toe-saw-rus)
- *Euoplocephalus* (you-oh-plo-keff-allus)
- *Hadrosaurus* (had-row-saw-rus)
- *Hypacrosaurus* (hi-pack-row-saw-rus)
- *Iguanodon* (ig-wan-oh-don)
- *Kritosaurus* (krit-oh-saw-rus)
- *Lambeosaurus* (lam-bay-oh-saw-rus)
- *Maiasaura* (my-ah-saw-rah)
- *Parasaurolophus* (para-saw-rol-oh-fus)
- *Plateosaurus* (plat-ay-oh-saw-rus)
- *Prosaurolophus* (pro-saw-rol-oh-fus)
- *Saurolophus* (saw-rol-oh-fus)
- *Triceratops* (try-ser-rah-tops)
- *Tyrannosaurus rex* (tie-ran-oh-saw-rus recks)

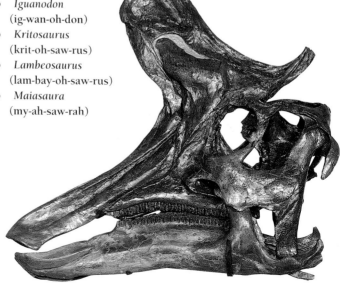

INDEX

ACKNOWLEDGMENTS

Picture credits
t=top b=bottom m=middle l=left r=right
Courtesy Department of Library Services,
American Museum of Natural History: Neg.
no. 37243, 11tl; Neg. no. 18502, 11ml; Neg. no.
18547, 12m; Neg. no. 18552, 12br–13bl; Neg.
no. 19488, 13tr; Neg. no. 19493, 13mr; Neg.
no. 18552, 29ml. Sternberg files, M. Walker
Collection; University Archives/Forsyth Library;
Fort Hays State University, Hays, Kansas: 12ml,
13tl. Bruce Coleman/Mark N. Boulton: 21mr.
Bridgeman Art Library: 21br.
   Model photography by Dave King: 2–7, 8,
9ml, 16, 17, 19b, 22–25, 26b, 28bl, 29br.
Museum photography by Lynton Gardiner:
10bl, 13br, 14–15, 18b, 20tr, 21tl, 23bl,
23br, 26mr, 28br, (bone) 29mr.

   Additional special photography by Paul
Bricknell (magnifying glass): 11tr,
29mr; Andy Crawford: (children)
5br, 14tr, 14bl, 15tr, 15br, 26b;
Jerry Young: (crocodile) 9tl.
   Index by Lynn Bresler.
   Dorling Kindersley would like
to thank Katherine Rogers for her
help in researching images from the
Sternberg files at Fort Hays State
University, Kansas. Thanks also to
Scarlett Lovell and Barbara Mathe
of the AMNH, as well as Charlotte
Holton for her knowledge of specimens;
Lowell Dingus and Fred Conrad for
their photography; and Perle A. of the
Mongolian Natural History Museum.

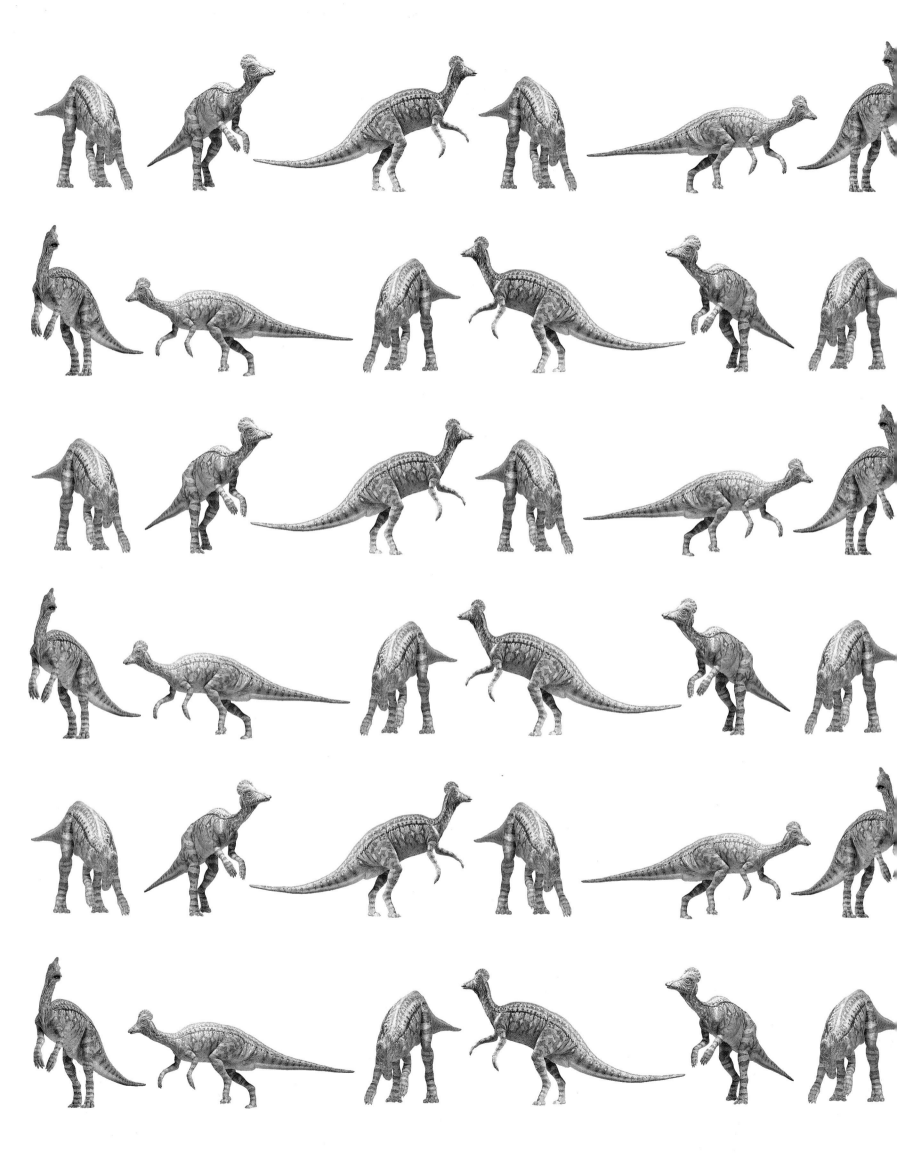